Genghis Khan

The Brave Warrior Who Bridged East and West

Story and Illustrations: Li Jian
Translation: Yijin Wert

Editorial Assistant: Zhang Mengke
Editors: Yang Xiaohe, Anna Nguyen
Editorial Director: Zhang Yicong

ISBN: 978-1-60220-991-6

Address any comments about *Genghis Khan: The Brave Warrior Who Bridged East and West* to:

Shanghai Press and Publishing Development Co., Ltd.
Floor 5, No. 390 Fuzhou Road, Shanghai, China (200001)
Email: sppd@sppdbook.com

Printed in China by Shanghai Donnelley Printing Co., Ltd.

3 5 7 9 10 8 6 4

Genghis Khan

The Brave Warrior Who Bridged East and West

by Li Jian

Translated by Yijin Wert

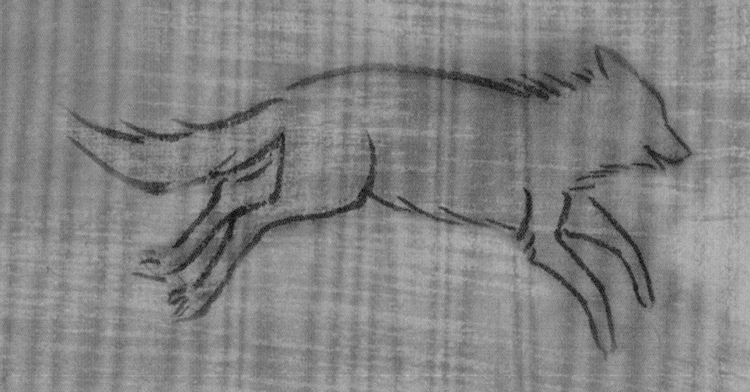

Better Link Press

In the 12th century on the Mongolian Plateau, a series of wars created unrest among the tribes causing them to frequently split up. Left without homes and little food, these people prayed for a leader who could end the continuous wars.

12世纪的蒙古高原，战争连年不断，部落四分五裂。人们流离失所、食不果腹，他们期盼着出现一位英雄，结束旷日持久的战争。

In 1162, a healthy and strong little baby boy was born in a small tribe near the Onon River. His father named him Temüjin. He hoped that someday the little boy would follow in his footsteps to become the chieftain of the tribe.

1162年，在鄂嫩河畔的一个小部落里，一个健壮的小男孩诞生了。父亲为他起名铁木真，希望有一天小男孩能追随自己的脚步，继承汗位。

Temüjin's father tragically passed away when he was very young.

不幸的是，铁木真的父亲在他很小的时候就去世了。

Temüjin claimed his father's position, but the people refused to be led by a boy. They wanted to leave Temüjin's family and find a leader somewhere else.

A tribe member led all the sheep away. As a young boy, Temüjin was unable to stop him.

铁木真称自己是父亲的继承人，可族人不愿意跟随一个年幼的男孩。他们要离开铁木真一家，另找别的首领依靠。

一个族人要把绵羊都赶走。铁木真只是个孩子，没能力阻止。

Another tribe member took all of the horses away. Temüjin asked him to stay, but he wouldn't listen.

另一个族人要把骏马都带走。铁木真要求他留下来，可是他不听。

Lastly, the rest of the tribe members left the family behind. They only viewed Temüjin as a young boy and couldn't be convinced to stay.

最后，剩下的族人也都离开了。他们只把铁木真当成一个孩子，不愿被说服留下来。

Temüjin's family was left with nothing. They lived in poverty, surviving primarily by picking wild fruits and hunting small game.

As the eldest male in the family, a determined Temüjin made plans to rebuild his tribe.

铁木真一家变得一无所有。他们生活困苦，只能靠摘野果、捕食小动物维持生活。

作为家里最年长的男性，铁木真发誓要重振自己的部落。

In order to fulfill his oath, Temüjin spent hours each day practicing archery. He became so skillful that he could hit a target from hundreds of steps away.

为了实现自己的誓言，铁木真每天坚持练习射箭。他的箭法超群，能在百步以外射中靶心。

Temüjin walked throughout the plateau to study war tactics. The wolves taught him how to attack enemies.

铁木真走遍了高原，学习战争战术。狼群教会了他袭击敌人的技巧。

Temüjin also wanted to improve his horse-riding skills, but he could not afford a horse. He could only dream of the wind running through his hair as he galloped on a powerful steed. On the Mongolian Plateau, a person without a horse was like a person without feet. What could he do?

铁木真还想学习骑术，可是他没有马。他只能想象着自己骑着骏马疾驰，想象着风儿吹拂头发的感觉。在蒙古高原，没有马就等于没有腿，这可怎么办呢？

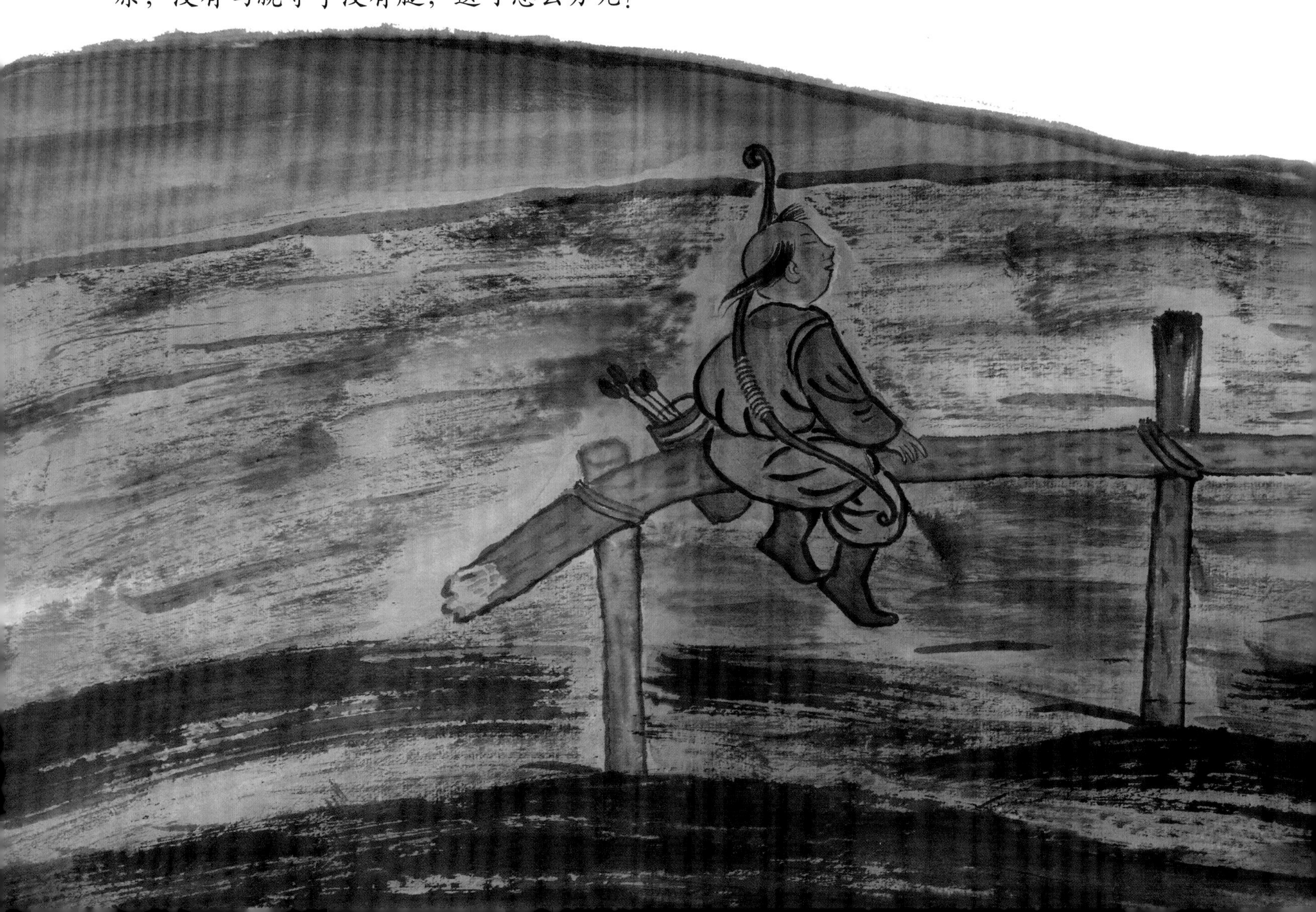

One day, Temüjin found several horses. He wanted to capture them to practice his riding skills. Temüjin's half-brother, Bekhter, also saw the horses. He thought it would be better to raise them as livestock. Temüjin got into a fight with his half-brother because they couldn't agree.

有一天，铁木真发现了几匹马，他想要捉住它们练习骑术。铁木真同父异母的兄弟别克帖儿也发现了这几匹马，他想要捉住它们当牲畜饲养。兄弟俩没能统一意见，在草原上厮打起来。

Temüjin's mother became very angry when she found out about the fight between the brothers. She taught them the need for alliances, but young Temüjin would not listen to her.

铁木真的母亲知道两兄弟打架后很生气。她告诉他们要团结，可是年轻的铁木真根本听不进去。

To help him understand, Temüjin's mother gave him an arrow and asked him if he could break it. Temüjin easily broke the arrow without any effort.

为了帮助孩子懂得道理，铁木真的母亲交给他一支箭，问他能不能折断。铁木真不费一点力气就折断了。

Then his mother gave him five arrows and asked if he could break them all together. Temüjin tried with all his might, but the arrows remained intact.

然后，铁木真的母亲又交给他五支箭，问他能不能折断。铁木真用尽了所有的力气，可箭束仍然完好如初。

Temüjin finally realized the meaning of his mother's lesson. The strength of five arrows was a lot more powerful than one. He needed to unite with his brothers to rebuild the tribe.

铁木真终于明白了母亲的教导的含义。五支紧紧捆在一起的箭要比一支强大得多。只有兄弟同心，才能重振部落。

In his adult life, Temüjin always remembered his mother's lesson. He formed strong alliances with his brothers and supporters to take back his people and animals.

长大后的铁木真牢记母亲的教诲。他团结兄弟盟友，带回了族人，收回了牲畜。

Temüjin became so popular that many warriors joined his troupe. He led them through a series of wars which eventually united all of the tribes. He became the hero of the people. Out of respect, they referred to him as "Genghis Khan," which meant universal ruler.

铁木真的名字越来越响亮，很多勇士来投奔他。铁木真带领他们经过一系列战役，最终统一了各个部落，结束了连年的战争。他就是人民一直期盼着的英雄，被尊称为“成吉思汗”，意为世界的统治者。

Genghis Khan and his descendants went on to conquer most of the land of Eurasia.

Kublai Khan, one of his grandsons, became the founder of China's Yuan dynasty (1271–1368) and set Dadu (today's Beijing) as the capital. Genghis Khan was posthumously given the title of Emperor Taizu of Yuan.

后来，成吉思汗和他的子孙的疆土横跨亚欧大陆。

成吉思汗的孙子忽必烈建立了中国元朝（1271—1368），定都大都（今北京），尊已过世的成吉思汗为“元太祖”。

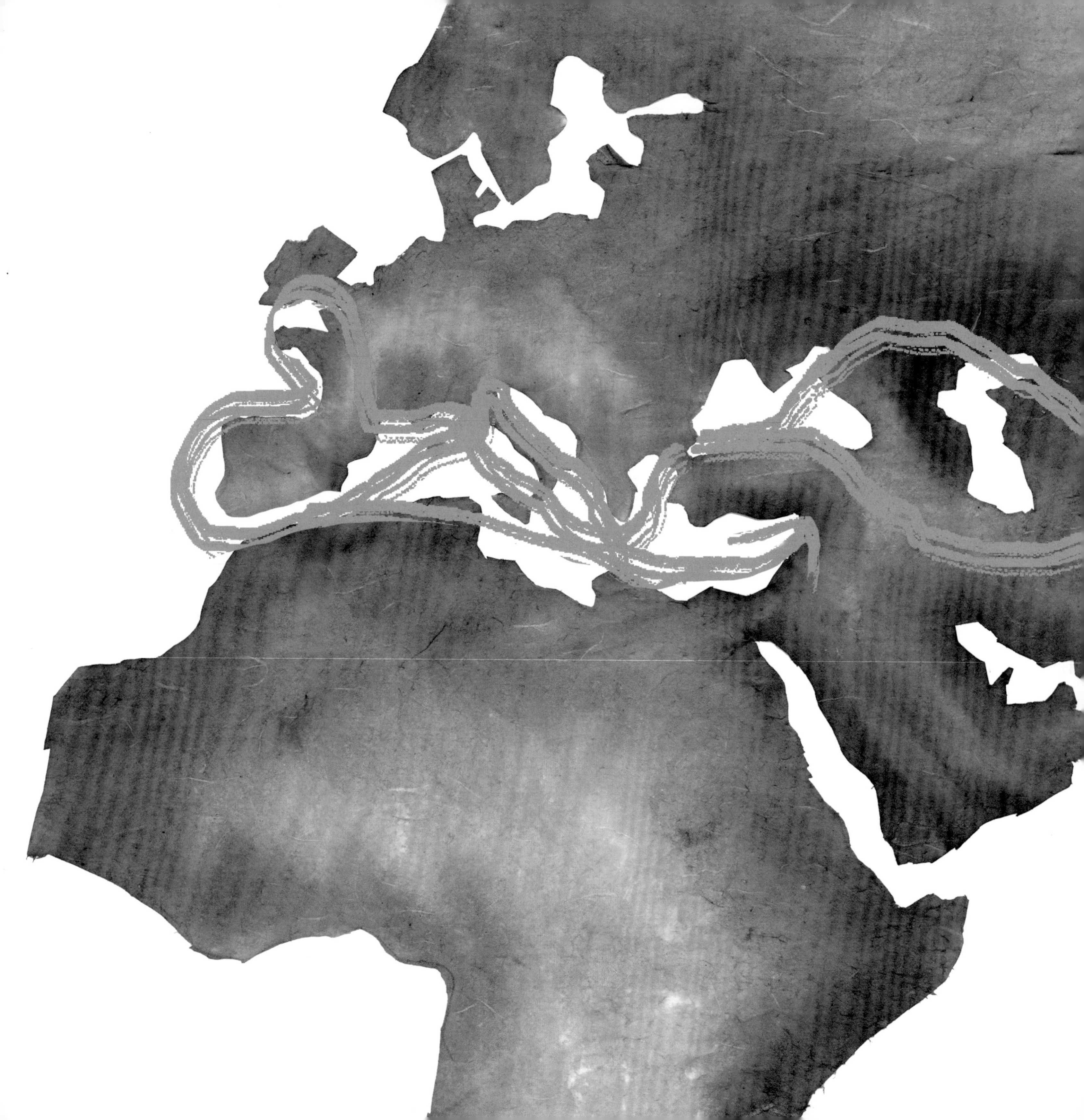

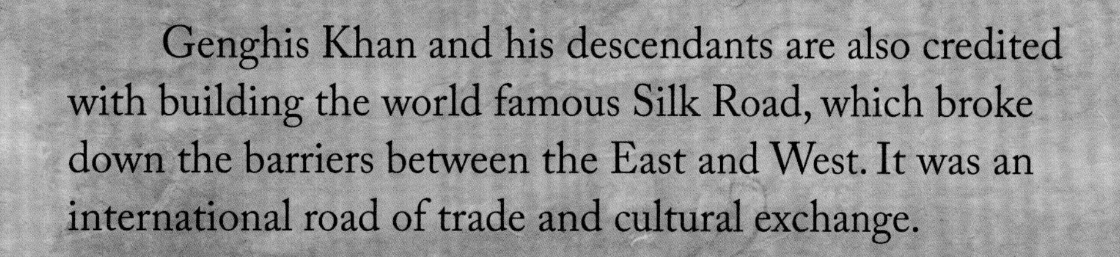

Genghis Khan and his descendants are also credited with building the world famous Silk Road, which broke down the barriers between the East and West. It was an international road of trade and cultural exchange.

成吉思汗和他的子孙们还开辟了闻名世界的丝绸之路。丝绸之路打通了东方和西方交流的壁垒，是一条国际性的商业和文化交流之路。

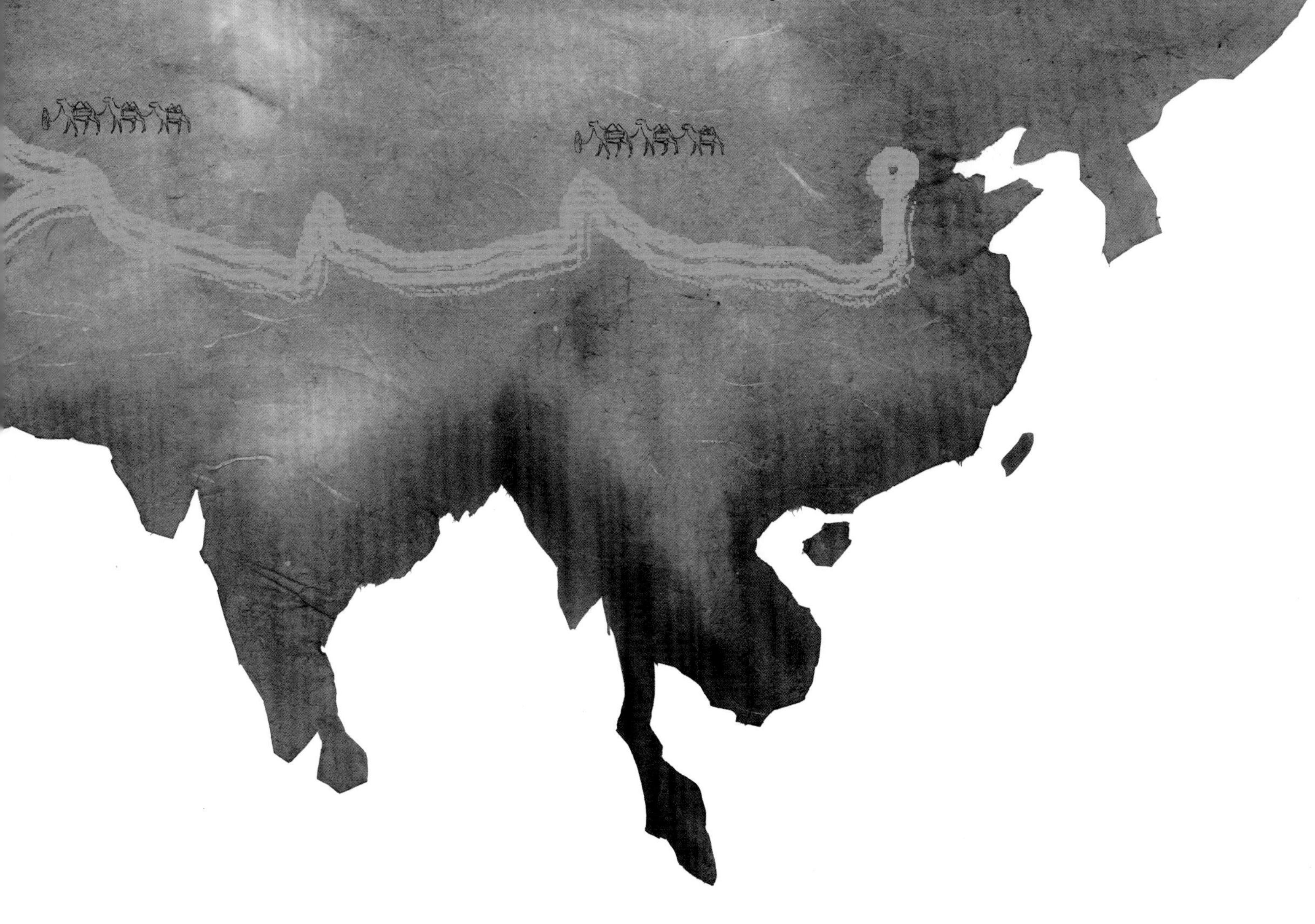

Cultural Explanation

Genghis Khan was an ancient Mongol leader, intelligent military commander, and a great politician. Originally named Temüjin, he was a descendant of the Borjigin clan. From the end of the 12th century to the beginning of the 13th century, he united the tribes under his Mongol confederation through a series of battles. In 1206, he became the emperor of the Mongol Empire and was declared Genghis Khan—meaning "universal ruler." After his grandson Kublai Khan became the founder of the Yuan dynasty (1271–1368), he placed his grandfather on the imperial records as Emperor Taizu, the official founder of the Yuan dynasty.

知识点

成吉思汗是古代蒙古首领、杰出的军事家和伟大的政治家。他原名铁木真，出生于孛儿只斤氏族。经过 12 世纪末 13 世纪初的一系列战役，他统一了蒙古各部落。1206 年他被推为蒙古汗国的大汗，称成吉思汗（意为世界的统治者）。他的孙子忽必烈建立元朝（1271–1368）后，追尊他为元太祖，意为元朝的开国之君。